7/07

Energy in Action™

HEAT

The Rosen Publishing Group's
PowerKids Press™
New York

Ian F. Mahaney

Published in 2007 by The Rosen Publishing Group, Inc.
29 East 21st Street, New York, NY 10010

First Edition

Editor: Joanne Randolph
Book Design: Julio Gil

Photo Credits: Cover, title page, p. 5 © Frithjof Hirdes/zefa/Corbis; p. 4 © Don Mason/Corbis; p. 7 © Tim Pannell/Corbis; p. 8 © www.istockphotos.com/Victor Kapas; p. 9 Maura B. McConnell; p. 11 © Roy Morsch/Corbis; p. 12 © www.istockphotos.com/Bill Shaw; p. 14 © Artville; p. 16 Cindy Reiman; p. 19 © www.istockphotos.com/Angelafoto; p. 20, 21, 22 Scott Bauer for The Rosen Publishing Group.

Library of Congress Cataloging-in-Publication Data

Mahaney, Ian F.
  Heat / Ian F. Mahaney.— 1st ed.
      p. cm. — (Energy in action)
  Includes index.
  ISBN (10) 1-4042-3477-2 (13) 978-1-4042-3477-2 (lib. bdg.) —
ISBN (10) 1-4042-2186-7 (13) 978-1-4042-2186-4 (pbk.)
  1. Heat—Juvenile literature. I. Title. II. Energy in action (PowerKids Press)
QC256.M34 2007
536—dc22
                                    2005029476

Manufactured in the United States of America

CONTENTS

Energy

Have you ever heard someone say that he or she has a lot of **energy**? Have you ever wondered what it means to have energy? Having energy means that you are able to accomplish something. When you have energy, you can climb a mountain or read a hard book.

"Energy" is an important word in science. In science energy is the ability to do work. There are many kinds of energy, from chemical energy to thermal, or heat, energy. Thermal energy is energy that causes **atoms** to move faster. This faster movement creates heat.

Opposite: Energy gives people the ability to do such things as climb mountains. People get their energy from food, which is chemical energy. *Above:* When fire, wood, and a gas called oxygen combine, they give off thermal energy.

Creating Heat

Rub your hands together. First rub them slowly until you feel them warm up. Then rub them faster. Do you feel them getting hotter? The faster you rub your hands together, the more heat they create.

Atoms also create heat when they move fast around one another. Atoms are the tiny parts that make up everything on Earth. They make up your skin, your shoe, and a pot of water on the stove. Atoms are always spinning and swirling around one another. The faster the atoms that make up an object move, the hotter that object becomes.

Rubbing your hands together on a cold day can help warm them. If you blow on your hands, it can help warm them, too. You are using the heat inside your body to give your hands more heat.

Measuring Heat

If you have ever helped bake cookies in an oven, you have probably felt how much heat the oven creates. However, the cookies would not turn out well if we cooked them based on how hot the oven feels. Instead we set the oven to a certain **temperature**. Temperature measures how hot or cold something is.

There are two common temperature scales. The **Celsius** scale is based on the boiling and **freezing** points of water. In the Celsius scale, water boils at 100 **degrees** (°) and freezes at 0°. Using the **Fahrenheit** scale, which is most often used in the United States, water boils at 212° and freezes at 32°.

Opposite: Temperature is measured using a tool called a thermometer. *Above:* We depend on heat energy to cook our food. This father and daughter are preparing to bake a cake in the oven.

The Science of Heat

When you boil a pot of water, the water inside the pot gets hot. If you carefully put your hand above the pot, you can feel that the air above the pot is hot, too. The heat from the pot of boiling water makes the cool air above the pot hotter. This is how heat operates. When two objects are set next to one another, heat flows from the hotter object to the cooler object. In the end the two objects will be the same temperature. This is called **heat transfer**. There are three types of heat transfer. They are **conduction**, **convection**, and **radiation**.

As water is heated to its boiling point, steam rises above the pot. This steam is water that has become hot enough to turn into a gas, or vapor. The water vapor transfers some of its heat to the surrounding air. When it becomes the same temperature as that air, we will no longer be able to see the steam.

Conduction

Conduction is one type of heat transfer. In conduction a hot object directly heats a cooler object. If you come inside after playing in the snow, your hands will probably be cold. When you put your cold hands into warm water, the water warms your hands. They are warmed directly by the water. This is an example of conduction. A burner on the stove heats a pan by conduction, too. Animals also use conduction. For example, a snake heats its body by conduction when it lies on a warm rock. Can you think of other examples in which heat transfers by means of conduction?

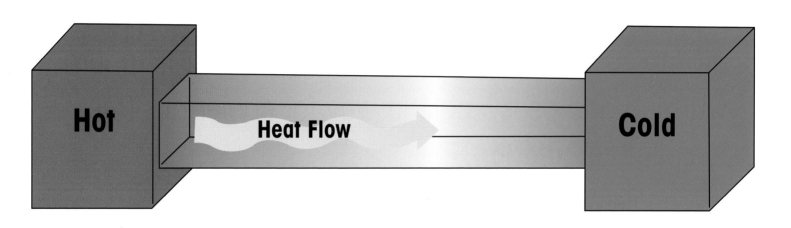

Hot

Heat Flow

Cold

Opposite: This lizard is sunning itself on a rock. Lizards and other reptiles, such as snakes, are cold-blooded animals. They need to use the heat energy from the Sun to warm their bodies.
Above: This picture shows how heat transfer by conduction works. The red box on the left is hot, and the blue one on the right is cold. The heat flows, or moves, from the hot area to the cold one.

Convection

The second type of heat transfer is convection. A boiling pot of water warming the air that surrounds it is an example of convection. In convection air that has been warmed rises. As the warm air rises, cool air moves in to take its place. This cool air is in turn warmed and rises, making way for cooler air. This is called **circulation**.

A heater used during winter warms the air by convection, too. **Cumulonimbus** clouds are also examples of convection. Warm air rises through the center of a cumulonimbus cloud. When this air meets the cold air higher up, the warm air loses some of its heat and falls back down.

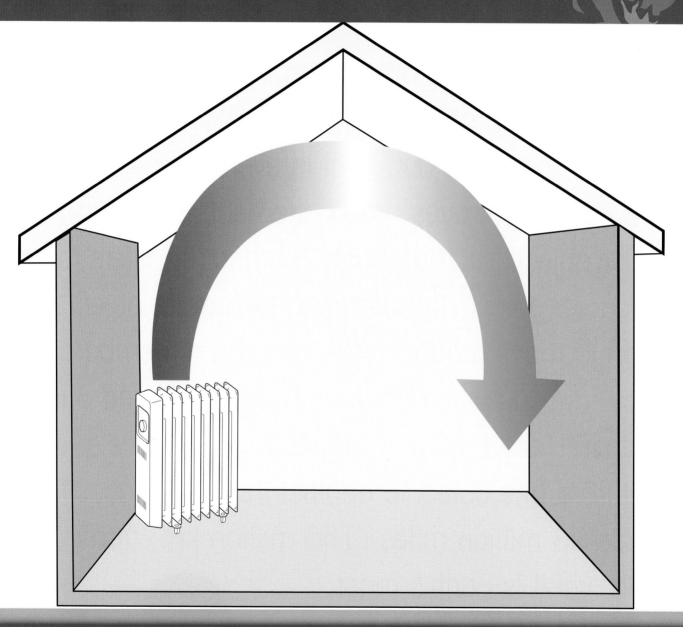

Opposite: Cumulonimbus clouds usually form during thunderstorms. *Above:* This picture shows how a room is heated by convection. As hot air comes from the heater, it moves up and away from the heater, toward cooler areas of the room. As the hot air moves away from the heater, it begins to lose some of its heat, and it falls. The air in the room circulates until an even temperature is reached.

Radiation

The Sun is an example of the third type of heat transfer, called radiation. The Sun is very hot. It **radiates**, or sends out, heat in every direction. The heat travels in waves. When the heat reaches a cooler object, such as Earth, the heat transfers to the cooler object. The atoms in the cooler object begin to move around faster. Do you remember what happens when atoms move fast around one another? They heat up. Radiation is the transfer of heat from one object to another through space. The Sun is 93 million miles (150 million km) from Earth, yet it is Earth's most important source of heat.

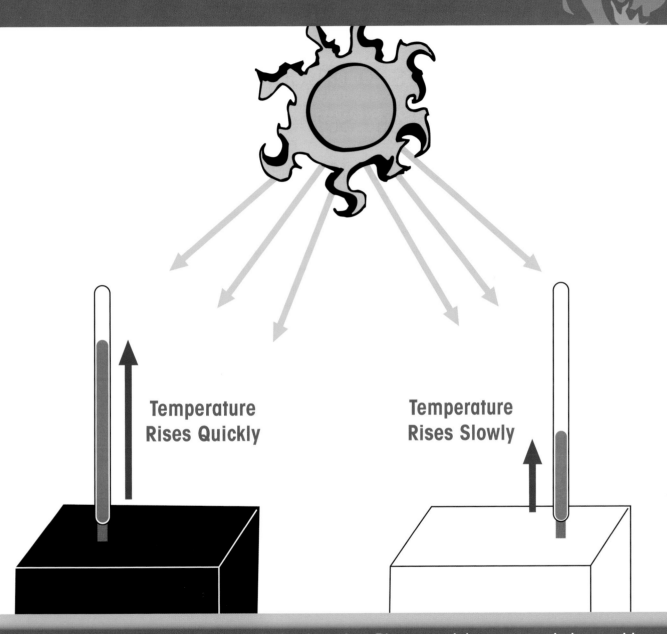

Temperature Rises Quickly

Temperature Rises Slowly

Opposite: You can see heat transfer by radiation in action. Place a rock in a sunny window and leave it there for an hour. Does it feel warmer? *Above:* This diagram shows that as radiation from the Sun hits a dark object, it gets hot quickly. This is because dark colors take in the energy from sunlight. The sunlight reflects, or bounces off, the light-colored object, so it takes longer for it to heat up.

Heat Capacity

When heat transfers to an object, the temperature of that object increases. Some objects need more heat than others for their temperature to increase. This is called **heat capacity**.

Did you know that the heat capacity of water is greater than that of most metals? It sounds surprising, but it is true! When you heat a pot of water on the stove, the pot becomes hot more quickly than the water does. This is because it takes more energy to heat up the water. The next time you cook food or feel sunlight on your face, think about what you have learned about heat!

Water's high heat capacity is what keeps the temperature on Earth from getting too hot or too cold. Earth's oceans take in most of the light and heat that reach Earth from the Sun. The temperature of the ocean does not rise very much, though. This keeps our weather and temperatures steady.

Experiments with Heat: Make a Thermometer

SUPPLIES NEEDED:

A clear, bendable tube, 1 foot (30.5 cm) long and 2 inches (5 cm) across (available at hardware stores), two stoppers to fit the tube ends, rubbing alcohol, food coloring, heavy string, a wire hanger, paper, a waterproof marker, rubber gloves and safety glasses or an adult, notebook and pen

A thermometer is the tool we use to measure how hot or cold something is. We use it to find out the temperature of our bodies or the air outside. In this experiment, you will make your own thermometer for use outside.

Step 1 Use 1 foot (30.5 cm) of tubing. Tightly plug one end of the tube with a stopper. This will be the bottom of the thermometer. Fill the tube halfway with rubbing alcohol. Wear safety gloves and glasses, or ask an adult for help.

Step 2 Add a small amount of red food coloring and put a stopper in the open end of the tube.

Step 3 Tie the thermometer to a tree and attach a piece of paper behind it with lines drawn 1 millimeter apart. You will use this to figure out the temperature.

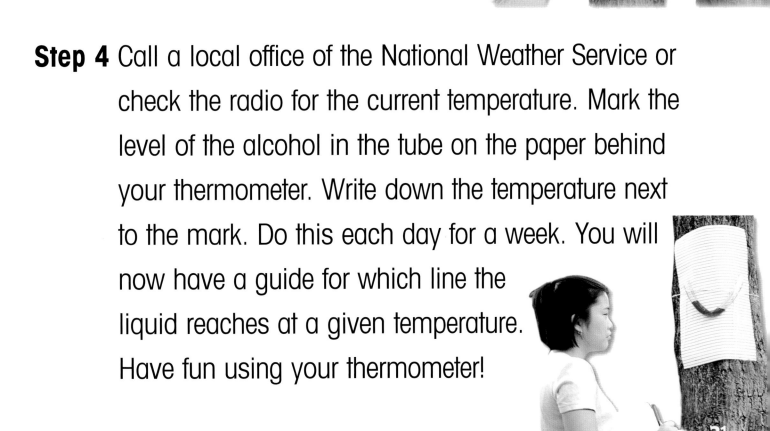

Step 4 Call a local office of the National Weather Service or check the radio for the current temperature. Mark the level of the alcohol in the tube on the paper behind your thermometer. Write down the temperature next to the mark. Do this each day for a week. You will now have a guide for which line the liquid reaches at a given temperature. Have fun using your thermometer!

Experiments with Heat: Keeping Warm

SUPPLIES NEEDED:

A large coffee can, 2 small cans, insulation (such as feathers, pillow fill, shredded cloth, and packing peanuts), a thermometer

Many animals that live in cold areas have insulation. Insulation is a layer of something that traps heat so it does not transfer to the cooler air outside. In this experiment you will test different kinds of insulation.

Step 1 Choose one kind of insulation and use it to fill a coffee can halfway. Fill a small can with hot tap water and place it in the center of the coffee can. Fill up the can with more insulation.

Step 2 Take the temperature of the water in the small can every minute for 5 minutes. Write the readings in your notebook. Do the same for each type of insulation you test. Which insulation keeps the water the warmest?

Glossary

atoms (A-temz) The smallest parts of elements that can exist either alone or with other elements.

Celsius (SEL-see-us) A scale that measures the freezing point of water as 0 degrees and the boiling point as 100 degrees.

circulation (ser-kyuh-LAY-shun) Movement from place to place.

conduction (kun-DUK-shun) The direct passing of heat from a warmer object to a cooler one.

convection (kun-VEK-shun) A type of heat transfer in which air is warmed and this warmed air circulates and warms the air around it.

cumulonimbus (kyoo-myuh-luh-NIM-bus) A thundercloud.

degrees (dih-GREEZ) Measurements of how hot or cold something is.

energy (EH-nur-jee) The power to work or to act.

Fahrenheit (FEHR-un-hyt) A scale that measures the freezing point of water as 32 degrees and the boiling point as 212 degrees.

freezing (FREEZ-ing) Making something so cold it becomes solid.

heat capacity (HEET kuh-PA-sih-tee) The amount of energy needed to raise the temperature of an object by one degree.

heat transfer (HEET TRANS-fer) Passing heat from one place or object to another.

radiates (RAY-dee-ayts) Spreads out from a center.

radiation (ray-dee-AY-shun) Rays of light, heat, or energy that spread outward from something.

temperature (TEM-pur-cher) How hot or cold something is.

Index

Web Sites

Due to the changing nature of Internet links, PowerKids Press has developed an online list of Web sites related to the subject of this book. This site is updated regularly. Please use this link to access the list: www.powerkidslinks.com/eic/heat/